The Great Cheese Robbery

For Mark and Annemarie,
who love elephants (and cheese)! – T W

First published in Great Britain in 2015 by Little Tiger Press Ltd

ISBN 978-0-545-84885-5

12 11 10 9 8 7 6 5 4 3 2 1   15 16 17 18 19 20/0

Printed in the U.S.A.   40

First Scholastic printing, February 2015

Disguises

The Great Cheese Robbery

Tim Warnes

SCHOLASTIC INC.

Daddy Elephant was as big
and strong as a tractor.
Patrick was small and only
a little bit strong.
Patrick was scared of lots
of things, like the dark,
ghosts, bees, and the fluff
you find under the sofa.

Daddy wasn't scared of anything.

Patrick tried and tried to make Daddy Elephant jump, but it never worked.

"It's not fair," sighed Patrick.
"You're not scared of anything!"

But there was **one** thing that scared
Daddy Elephant . . .

One afternoon there was a squeak at the door.

"Look, Daddy," gasped Patrick. "A teeny-tiny elephant!"

"That's not an elephant," cried Daddy.

IT'S A M-M-M-MOUSE!

"Good day, gentlemen,"
said the mouse. "My name
is Cornelius J. Parker,
from the Cheese Inspection
Council. I'm here to inspect
your cheese."

"W-w-we haven't got any,"
stammered Daddy Elephant.
  "Yes we have," said Patrick
helpfully, "in the fridge.
I'll show you."

Cornelius J. Parker made a very thorough inspection indeed.

Cornelius opened his briefcase and pulled out a walkie-talkie.

Soon there was another
squeak at the door.

"We're 'ere for the fridge,"
said a stocky mouse.

"The fridge?" asked Patrick.

"We're confiscating it on
grounds of health and
safety," said the skinny one.

"B-b-but I'm making macaroni cheese tonight," said Daddy.

"It's his signature dish," Patrick added.

"Not any more, it's not!" said Cornelius.

Mascarpone! Manchego! Follow me!

"Don't worry – I'll help!"
called Patrick.

Suddenly there was a loud cry from the lounge.

MORE M-M-M-MICE!

The mice had a sneaky plan.

and not just the fridge. The mice took the television, the phone, the fish, the biscuits, the lamp . . .

even Patrick's toys!

Daddy Elephant gave a little whimper as the mice cheered and lifted up the sofa.

STOP! THAT'S MY DADDY!

Patrick shouted in his biggest, strongest voice. But the mice did not notice.

Just at that moment . . .

. . . Mommy Elephant appeared.

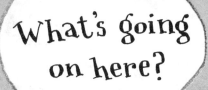

"Put my husband down OR ELSE!"
shouted Mommy Elephant.

Everybody froze.

Cornelius narrowed his eyes.
"Or else, what?"
    Patrick's Mommy took a big,
deep breath and . . .

"The truth is, Patrick," said Mommy Elephant, "everyone's afraid of something – even your big old dad!"

"But he's still the biggest, strongest elephant around," said Patrick.

"I am," smiled Daddy proudly. "But when it comes to mice . . .

Mommy's the bravest!"